Dolphin Bay

ROSIE BANKS

ORCHARD

This is the Secret Kingdom

Dolphin Bay

Book One

Contents

A Camping Trip

"Ouch!" squeaked Summer as Ellie accidentally jabbed her arm with a plastic spade.

"Sorry!" Ellie tucked the spade between a stripy beach ball and the picnic hamper, which was squashed against her legs on the floor of the car. "I was trying to get the sweets. Who wants a strawberry sherbet?"

"Me, please!" Summer and Jasmine chorused together.

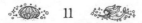

"Us too," said Molly, Ellie's little sister.
"Don't we, Caitlin?"

Ellie leaned forward to offer Molly and
her friend the packet, then passed them to
Summer and Jasmine, who were sitting on
either side of her.

"How ever did you manage to find
them amongst all our stuff?" asked
Jasmine, taking two sweets from the bag.
Every centimetre of the people carrier
was jam-packed with holiday things.
There were rucksacks, bright orange tents,
snuggly sleeping bags, a tiny cooking

stove, plastic spades and fishing nets. Ellie's parents were taking Ellie, her best friends Summer and Jasmine, and Molly and her friend Caitlin on a camping holiday by the seaside for a whole week.

"It was a tough job, but someone had to do it." Ellie grinned.

"How much further is it, Dad?" Molly sighed.

"Not long now," said Mr Macdonald. "Look out for the signs to the campsite."

"I wonder what it'll be like?" Summer pushed her long blonde plaits back over her shoulders. "Do you think we'll see dolphins swimming in the sea?"

"If we don't see dolphins then I'll make you a sand one," promised Ellie. Her green eyes sparkled with excitement. "I'll decorate it with shells and seaweed."

There was a faraway look on Jasmine's face. "I love the beach. It's like an enormous stage. I'm going to practise my new dance steps on it."

"We're going to have a brilliant time!" declared Ellie happily.

"Maybe even a magic time!" whispered Jasmine with a grin. She caught her friends' eyes. The three of them had an exciting secret. They looked after a magical box that had been made by the kindly King Merry, who was the ruler of an enchanted land called the Secret Kingdom. The Secret Kingdom was a very special place, where amazing creatures like pixies, elves and unicorns lived. Whenever there was trouble in the Secret Kingdom a message appeared in the Magic Box and Ellie, Summer

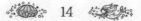

and Jasmine were whisked away to the kingdom to try and help. Usually it was because King Merry's horrible sister, Queen Malice, had been causing trouble.

Suddenly Molly squealed. "I see a sign!"

"Sunny Sands Campsite," Ellie read out. "We're here!"

The moment Mr Macdonald stopped the car and switched off the engine, Ellie, Summer and Jasmine unbuckled their seat belts and tumbled out. At the bottom of the hill was a hedge and beyond the hedge was the glittering blue sea!

"Look at the sea!" Jasmine cried. "It's beautiful." She twirled round on the grass, her long dark hair swinging around her. "This is so exciting."

"What can we do to help, Mrs Macdonald?" Summer asked. Molly and

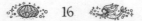

Caitlin had already run over to a patch
of grass and were doing cartwheels and
handstands.

"Should we start getting the tents out?"
Ellie asked. She opened the car boot and
immediately a jumble of bags fell out.
"Whoops!"

Summer and Jasmine quickly picked the
bags up.

"Maybe Dad and I would be better off

sorting everything out on our own," said Ellie's mum. "Why don't you three just go and explore? The beach is on the other side of that hedge, but keep away from the water."

"Okay. Thanks, Mum!" Ellie said.

"Race you both to the beach!" called Jasmine.

Ellie and Summer tore after her as she ran towards a gap in the hedge. They caught up with her and stepped onto the beach together.

"Isn't the sea beautiful,' said Ellie, looking at the waves lapping at the shore. "I want to get my paints out and paint a picture of it."

Jasmine twirled her round and laughed. "This is going to be the best holiday ever!" she cried.

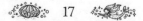

Summer's sandals sank into the soft sand and she sighed happily. "The sand's almost as pretty as the sand on Glitter Beach in the Secret Kingdom."

"Only this sand won't turn into magical dust!" said Ellie, thinking of Glitter Beach with its aquamarine sea, golden sand and little fairy shops surrounding it.

"Where's the Magic Box at the moment?" Jasmine asked curiously.

"In my rucksack back at the car," Ellie replied. Excitement tingled through her. She hoped they would be needed soon. She couldn't wait to visit the Secret Kingdom again.

As the girls started to walk along the beach, dodging the piles of seaweed on the sand, Ellie grinned as she thought of a joke. "Why did the crab blush?"

Jasmine and Summer raised their
eyebrows. "Why?"

"Because the sea*weed*," giggled Ellie.

Jasmine and Summer groaned loudly.

With Ellie telling every sea or fish joke
she could think of, the three of them
explored the beach and rock pools. When
they finally got back to the campsite they
saw that Ellie's parents had been very
busy. There was a big tent standing with
its entrance facing in the direction of the
beach. Next to it was a smaller one where
the food and cooking things were being
kept. The door was tied back and inside
there were lots of boxes filled with fresh
fruit and vegetables, pasta, tins, pots, pans
and cutlery. Outside the tents was a picnic
table with seven chairs. It was covered
with a huge striped umbrella to keep the

sun off everyone while they were eating.
Mrs Macdonald waved at the girls from
the entrance of the main tent. "Come
inside and look at your room."

Summer was puzzled. "We have a room
in a tent?"

"Oh, yes," smiled Mrs Macdonald.
"Come and see."

The tent was tall enough for Ellie's

mum to stand up in. Excitedly the girls crowded inside. There were five sections – a large square area in the middle with two smaller rooms on the left and two more on the right.

"This must be our room," said Ellie, pulling back a piece of orange material and stepping into the first room on the left. "It's got our sleeping bags in."

She sat down on her green and purple sleeping bag.

"Wow!" said Jasmine, sitting cross-legged on her pink and lilac sleeping bag.

"Double wow!" agreed Summer,
carefully picking up a ladybird crawling
along her rainbow-coloured bed. "And
I've already found a pet!"

Ellie and Jasmine laughed as Summer
carefully carried the ladybird outside.
Summer loved all animals, no matter how
small!

"Let's unpack," said Ellie, reaching for
her rucksack. She unzipped the top and
pulled out the Magic Box, which she'd
covered with bubble wrap to keep it safe.
The bubbles seemed to be sparkling in
the sunshine. Ellie frowned, then started
pulling the bubble wrap off as fast as
she could, making lots of little popping
sounds.

"What are you doing?" Summer asked.

"Look!" Ellie pulled the final piece of

bubble wrap off and held the box up. It shone and glittered, light dancing across its mirrored surface.

Jasmine caught her breath. "The box is glowing! King Merry must need our help."

"I wonder what the problem is this time," said Summer anxiously.

Ellie's eyes shone. "There's only one way to find out!"

Return to the Secret Kingdom

The girls watched as words appeared on the glowing lid of the Magic Box. Ellie started to read them out. "Look for a..."

"Wait, Ellie!" Jasmine interrupted, holding up her hand. "We can't read the message out here. What if Molly or Caitlin or one of your parents came in? We need to go somewhere quieter."

Ellie realised Jasmine was right. "Let's go back to the beach." She wrapped the box in a beach towel and they hurried outside.

"Don't be out too long, girls," Mrs Macdonald called. "I'm just getting lunch ready."

"Okay, Mum," said Ellie, feeling very glad that whenever the girls went to the Secret Kingdom no time passed in their own world. Mum would never even know they'd gone!

When they reached the beach they headed for a cluster of rocks. They all kneeled down behind the largest rock. The mirrored lid of the Magic Box was still glowing brightly, light spilling out onto the pictures of unicorns, mermaids and elves carved into its sides. Ellie read out the riddle that was shining in the lid.

"Look for a cove not far away,
Where all the dolphins come to play."

The lid of the box sprang open and a
piece of paper floated out in a shower
of sparkles. The girls leaned in closer as
the magic map unfolded, showing the
crescent moon-shaped island laid out as if
they were looking down on it through a
window.

"If we're looking for dolphins it will have to be somewhere with water," said Ellie. "There's a lake here," she added, pointing to the map.

"A lake won't be right. Dolphins live in the sea. And we're meant to look for a cove..." Summer's eyes searched the pictures. "How about there?" She pointed at a pretty cove. There was a golden beach and a large, old-fashioned sailing ship floating in the aquamarine water. Dolphins and mermaids were swimming around the ship. The mermaids waved at the girls.

"Dolphin Bay," said Jasmine, reading the label on the map. "I bet that's where we need to go!"

Eagerly the girls laid their hands on each of the six green stones decorating

the lid of the Magic Box.

"Dolphin Bay!" they whispered hopefully.

There was a flash of light followed by a tinkling laugh. The girls' eyes flew open.

"Trixi!" they all exclaimed.

A pretty pixie with messy blonde hair was hovering in the air on a leaf. She was wearing a flowery pink and silver swimming costume, silver sandals covered with gemstones and a big floppy sunhat made out of a daisy.

"Hello, girls," Trixi cried as she swooped closer. "It's so good to see you again!"

"What's the problem in the Secret Kingdom this time?" asked Ellie anxiously.

Trixi laughed. "It's all right. There's no problem. We're having our summer holiday at Dolphin Bay and King Merry would love you to join us. Would you like to?"

"Oh, yes please!" said Ellie, Summer and Jasmine together.

"Will there really be dolphins?" Summer gasped. "I'd love to swim with them."

"There'll be lots and lots of dolphins," said Trixi. "And of course you can swim with them. They'd like that. They're very friendly." She grinned, then she tapped her pixie ring and sang out:

"For a sunny holiday,
Take us now to Dolphin Bay."

The girls quickly grabbed one another's hands as green and gold sparkles shot from Trixi's pixie ring and twirled around them. As the sparkles spun faster and faster they felt themselves being magically whisked away.

Ellie landed with a bump. She realised that the ground beneath her was moving and the air smelled salty. Where were they? She opened her eyes.

"We're on a ship," she gasped, blinking.

It was the old-fashioned ship they'd seen on the map. Strings of bunting were stretched between the three masts, and from the tallest one flew a huge purple flag with a golden crown in the centre.

"And we've got our tiaras on!" said Summer, touching the silver tiara that had appeared on her head. Their tiaras always appeared when they arrived in the Secret Kingdom to show that they were Very Important Friends of King Merry.

"Look!" Jasmine pointed to five curly blue flumes that led from the ship's deck, twisting down into the sea. Elves wearing brightly coloured swimming costumes were whizzing down them, leaning sideways as they sped round the corners and then shooting into the sea.

"That looks like fun,' said Ellie.

"And there are mermaids in the water!" breathed Summer. Beautiful mermaids were swimming in the sea, laughing and clapping, their long brightly coloured hair sweeping through the water and their silvery tails splashing.

"Can we go on the slides?" Jasmine asked Trixi.

"Of course, but why don't you come and say hello to King Merry first," said Trixi. "He's having a swim. He'll be thrilled that you're here."

The girls followed her leaf as it zoomed across the deck of the boat. Ellie's head turned this way and that as she tried to take everything in.

"Look at those seahorses," she said, pointing to a cluster of model seahorses made out of shining silver metal. They

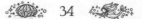

had long delicate noses.
As the girls passed,
water sprayed out
of the seahorses'
mouths. All three
girls squealed as it
sprayed over them.
It was like being
caught in a sprinkler
at home!

Trixi had darted out of the way just in
time. She giggled at the girls' surprised
faces. "Sorry! I should have warned you
about that! It's just one of King Merry's
little jokes."

The girls didn't mind being wet. The
sun was already drying their skin. It was
just so much fun to be there! Ellie spotted
something on the other side of the boat.

"Look at that octopus. It's giving rides!"

A giant orange octopus was swimming across the sea. Chairs were strapped to four of its long legs, and in each chair sat a giggling elf.

"And look! There's a ice cream boat!" said Jasmine, pointing to where a jolly-looking elf was rowing around the bay, handing out huge multicoloured ice creams.

"I've heard of an ice cream van before, but never an ice cream *boat!*" giggled Ellie, amazed.

"And there's King Merry!" cried Summer in delight as she spotted the jolly king floating around in the water in a giant rubber ring. "King Merry!" she called, waving.

"Summer! Jasmine! Ellie! How wonderful to see you!" King Merry waved at them so happily that his rubber ring overturned and he landed in the water with a splash!

"Oopsy daisy!" laughed Trixi, zooming down to help him. Jasmine, Ellie and Summer rushed up to the railing at the edge of the deck.

Ellie giggled as she looked at the kindly king splashing in the glittering aquamarine water. This looked like it was going to be their best trip to the Secret Kingdom yet!

Fun in the Sea

With Trixi's help, King Merry was soon
back in his rubber ring, which was
decorated with pictures of castles and
crowns. He was wearing a red and white
old-fashioned bathing suit, and next
to him floated a smaller rubber ring
containing a tall pink drink. The drink
was piled high with pieces of fruit and
had a long curly straw that twisted and
looped like a helter skelter slide.

When the girls leaned over the rail and waved at him, King Merry's rosy face broke into a huge smile. "Goodness gracious me! I'm so glad you could make it here for the Dolphin Dances."

"Dolphin Dances?" echoed Jasmine.

But King Merry didn't explain any more. "Why don't you put your costumes on and join in the fun?"

"We didn't bring our swimming costumes," Summer whispered to Ellie and Jasmine in alarm.

"I can sort that out," said Trixi, flying her leaf back up to them. She tapped her ring and the next instant the girls found themselves wearing pretty swimming costumes. Ellie's was green with purple flowers, Summer's was decorated with multicoloured butterflies and Jasmine's

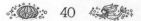

was bright pink with tiny
gold polka dots. She
did a twirl.

"I love this," she
said excitedly.
"Thank you, Trixi."

Trixi whizzed about
on her leaf. "Now let's
go and have some fun!"

Ellie looked around. "What shall we do
first?" There was so much to choose from!

"I'm going on the flumes," said Jasmine.

"Me too!" said Ellie. They set off across
the deck, but Summer stayed where she
was. She liked swimming but she didn't
really like getting her face wet or going
underwater.

"Are you coming?" Jasmine asked,
looking back over her shoulder.

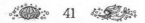

"You go," Summer said. "I think I'll...I'll...explore the boat for a bit."

"It's okay, Summer. We don't have to go on the flumes," Ellie said kindly, realising what the matter was.

"No, you two go on. I'll be fine!" Summer urged. "I know you both love water slides, and I'm sure I can get into the water another way."

"Oh, yes. That's easy!" said Trixi. She tapped her ring and the next minute Summer found herself whizzing through the air and landing in a rubber ring of her own. She bobbed up and down in the water, gasping in astonishment.

"Oh, wow!" she exclaimed. "Thanks, Trixi!" she called up as the

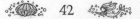

pixie whizzed down beside her.

"No problem!" said the pixie, grinning as she hovered on her leaf by Summer's head.

"Come and join us!" Summer beckoned to her friends, who were still up on the deck.

Jasmine and Ellie ran to the flumes. Soon they were whizzing down them, going round and round, faster and faster until they shot out into the water, squealing.

Summer grinned as they surfaced, shaking the water droplets from their hair before heading straight back to the ship for another turn. It was wonderful watching everything that was going on – the squealing elves, the smiling mermaids, the big octopus...

Just then, a beautiful mermaid with rainbow-coloured hair popped out of the sea beside Summer's ring. "Hello, I'm Marika," she said. "Are you Summer, Jasmine or Ellie?"

"I'm Summer," Summer replied.

"It's lovely to meet you, Summer," said the mermaid. "I've heard all about you three girls from Lady Merlana. You're all so brave."

Summer smiled. The girls had had a great adventure with Lady Merlana, the leader of the mermaids, when they saved the Wishing Pearl. "Is she here?"

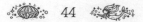

44

"No, not today." Marika swished her tail and swam round to the other side of the ring. "But I'll tell her I've met you. Are you enjoying Dolphin Bay?"

"Oh, yes!" said Summer happily. "It's so...so..." She struggled to find exactly the right word to say how perfect it was.

"Swishy?" said Marika.

Summer grinned. "Yes, it's very swishy!" She suddenly caught sight of something that made her heart leap. "Dolphins!" she cried, pointing. "Look! Over there by King Merry."

King Merry was surrounded by a large group of friendly grey dolphins. *A pod*, Summer thought, remembering the proper name for a group of dolphins.

"Look!" Summer called to Ellie and Jasmine as they slid down the flume and

splashed into the water next to her. The others gasped as they spotted the dolphins.

"Let's go over!" Jasmine said excitedly.

Summer tipped herself off her rubber ring and slid into the cool sea. "Bye, Marika!" Keeping her head above the water, she swam with the others towards King Merry and the dolphins.

"Ah, girls, you must meet the dolphins!" cried King Merry as he saw them.

The dolphins greeted them with happy clicks and whistling sounds.

"Oh, wow," Summer breathed as the beautiful creatures swam up and nuzzled her. They were all so sleek and smooth, their grey skin shining in the sun.

"These are the dolphins who live here in the bay," King Merry said. "This is Happy." A dolphin with a wide smile leaped out of the water in a flurry of water droplets.

"Hello!" he called out in a musical voice, before plunging back into the sparkling sea.

"And this is Silver." Another dolphin jumped into the air, his body gleaming silver in the sunlight as he turned a

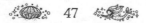

somersault. "And Flash…"

The king rattled off a list of names and each dolphin jumped or twisted or somersaulted as his or her name was called out. Finally, the king announced, "And these are the newest members of the dolphin pod, Bubbles and Splash."

Two adorable baby dolphins swam forward and kissed each of the girls on

the cheek with their blunt grey noses.

"I'm Bubbles," said one, her dark eyes shining. "Is this your first time at the Dolphin Dances?"

"Yes," said the girls.

"It's our first time too," piped up Splash, bobbing his head. "We're really looking forward to it."

"What exactly are the Dolphin Dances?" Jasmine asked.

"They're amazing," whistled Bubbles excitedly. "Dolphins from all around the Secret Kingdom gather here in the bay to dance together—"

"Yes," Splash interrupted. "The Dolphin Dances are a way of sharing the stories of things that dolphins have done in the past. Whenever something important happens we make up a dance about it. Then, every

year, all the dolphins in the Secret
Kingdom come here and learn the
different dances so that the stories will
always be remembered."

"Like a history lesson," said Ellie.

Jasmine grinned. "I wish our history
lessons at school
involved
dancing!"

"And
dolphins!"
giggled
Summer.

Splash nudged
Summer with his
nose. "The other dolphins haven't got here
yet. Would you like to play with us until
they arrive?"

"Please say yes!" Bubbles splashed the

water with her silvery tail.

Ellie, Jasmine and Summer grinned at each other. "Oh, yes!"

Hide and Squeak

"I'd better get back on board and prepare for the arrival of the other dolphins," King Merry said as the girls started to play with Bubbles and Splash. "But do have fun. Will you help me, Trixi?"

"Of course, Your Majesty," she smiled. "I'll see you later!"

"Let's play hide and seek," said Bubbles eagerly. "You three hide and we'll find you."

"We'll count to twenty and then shout 'Dolphin Dances are Forever!' before we come and find you," said Splash.

The baby dolphins shut their eyes tight and began slowly counting to twenty. Grinning at each other, Ellie, Summer and Jasmine swam away to hide. Jasmine swam over to King Merry's yacht. Ellie headed for the ice cream boat and Summer swam after her.

"Wait for me," she panted.

Giggling together, the girls hid behind the ice cream boat. Ellie pushed her hair away from her ears and listened hard, her heart beating fast with excitement. Suddenly she heard

Bubbles whistle, "Dolphin Dances are Forever!" followed by a huge splash as Bubbles and Splash dived down into the water.

"They're coming to find us," Ellie whispered to Summer. She dived under the water. Summer kept as low as she could. After a few seconds Ellie popped up again. "There's a strange clicking noise under the water. I wonder what it—"

She broke off as Bubbles shot up through the water next to them.

"Found you!" she cried, her mouth open in a wide grin.

"That was fast!" Ellie exclaimed.

Bubbles whistled as if she was laughing and just then Jasmine swam out from behind the yacht with Splash. "We found you all!" cried Splash.

"But how did you find us so quickly?" Jasmine asked.

The baby dolphins just winked at each other.

"Your go now!" said Splash.

It took Ellie, Summer and Jasmine much longer to find the dolphins. And the next time they hid the dolphins found them even faster.

At last Ellie groaned, "Okay, what's your secret? How come you're so good at this?"

"It's our sonar," giggled Splash.

"Oh! I should have guessed when Ellie

said she heard clicking under the water," Summer exclaimed. Seeing the baffled expressions on her friends' faces she added, "Lots of animals use sonar. It's a way of finding something with sound. Dolphins make a clicking noise and when the clicks hit a solid object they bounce back, like a reflection. The dolphins use the reflected sound to work out exactly where the object is."

"That's so clever," said Ellie.

"And a tiny bit cheaty," said Jasmine. With a cheeky giggle, she splashed water at the baby dolphin twins.

"Water fight!" whistled Bubbles, using her tail to splash Jasmine back.

Soon the water was foaming like a shaken bottle of fizzy drink as everyone joined in the water fight. Summer

squealed and swam off a little way as her
face got splashed but Ellie and Jasmine
dived around, throwing water over the
dolphins.

"This is such fun!"
hiccupped Jasmine
as she almost
swallowed some
sea water.

"Here I
come!" whistled
Bubbles, leaping
out of the water and
diving down beside Ellie, sending a wave
crashing over her head.

Ellie spluttered, shaking the water out of
her red curls. "Got you back!" she cried,
splashing Bubbles as the little dolphin
surfaced and squirted water out of her

blowhole. Bubbles opened her mouth and made a clicking, laughing sound.

Summer grinned as she watched them play, but suddenly her eyes were caught by movement further out in the sea. "Hey! Look over there!"

Ellie and Jasmine swung round and their mouths opened.

"It's the rest of the Secret Kingdom dolphins!" cried Splash, jumping out of the water and somersaulting with excitement. "Yippee!"

The girls stared in awe as they watched dozens of beautiful dolphins surging through the water and leaping over the waves, their bodies glinting in the sunlight.

Trixi swooped towards them on her leaf. "Everybody back on the royal yacht!" she called. "All aboard!"

"Bye, Bubbles! Bye, Splash!" Ellie called as the girls started to swim towards the nearest ladder. "See you later!"

"Bye!" whistled the baby dolphins.

The sea was suddenly full of splashes and laughter as all the elves that had been swimming in the bay clambered up the ladders and rushed for a place on the boat to watch the arrival of the dolphins.

King Merry was now at the enormous
wheel, steering the ship. The girls followed
Trixi over to
where he was
standing.

King
Merry tried
to steer the
ship over
to meet
the dolphins,
but they ended
up sailing in a big
circle instead! "Oh, I love the Dolphin
Dances!" he declared as they turned
around and around. "Just wait until you
see them perform."

Suddenly Ellie screwed up her eyes.
"What's that?"

Summer and Jasmine peered in the direction she was pointing. A dark shape was coming up behind the dolphins, moving fast.

"Fetch my telescope!" King Merry cried anxiously.

Trixi tapped her ring and a golden telescope appeared. King Merry looked through the eyepiece. Ellie had a funny feeling in her stomach, like butterflies were fluttering there. She glanced at Summer and Jasmine. What was that coming towards them?

King Merry groaned. "Oh, no!"

"What is it, Your Majesty?" asked Trixi.

"It's Queen Malice!" cried the king.

Disaster!

The girls all looked at each other in
alarm. The king's sister, Queen Malice,
was always causing trouble. She wanted
to be the ruler of the Secret Kingdom and
she loved making people unhappy. The
girls had managed to stop her evil plans
in the past, but if she was back she was
sure to be planning something horrible.
The elves huddled together, murmuring
anxiously, and the mermaids ducked deep
down under the water.

As the dark shape got closer, the girls saw that it was a high-backed chariot made of twisted black metal. It was covered in dripping seaweed and slime, and pulled by an enormous killer whale. Queen Malice stood tall and proud, seaweed reins in one hand, her black cloak and frizzy hair blowing out behind her as the chariot sped closer.

"Faster," she shrieked, thumping her black staff down on the chariot floor. "Faster, I say!" The sea water parted as her chariot ploughed closer towards the bay.

Ellie reached for Summer and Jasmine's hands as she spotted four familiar creatures flapping round the queen's head. Storm Sprites! They were Queen Malice's servants – nasty creatures with pointed

faces, grey skin and leathery wings.

"We're coming to get you!" they
screeched.

The killer whale turned sharply,
creating a small tidal wave as he stopped
the chariot in front of the royal ship.

"What is the meaning of this, sister? Why are you here?" demanded King Merry.

"To stop you having fun with your Dolphin Dances, of course!" Queen Malice hissed and pulled out an oyster shell from under her cloak.

"Oyster, grow, be giant in size,
Grow right now before my eyes."

Everyone gasped as the oyster started to grow and grow. With a cackle, the queen hurled it into the bay. The water churned violently as the giant oyster sank.

"Now see how much you like spending time here at Dolphin Bay!" shrieked Queen Malice. With a triumphant laugh she banged her staff on the floor of the

chariot. Immediately the killer whale turned round and took off, speeding back out of the bay.

"What did she do?" said Jasmine. "What was that oyster for?"

Before anyone could reply, the sea started to churn again. The dolphins burst out of the water, whistling in fear. The mermaids surfaced too, their faces screwed up and their hands over their ears. "Oh, ow! Ow!" they cried. "There's a dreadful noise under the water!"

"I can't bear it," squealed Bubbles.

"It's too loud!" whistled Squeak.

"I wonder what's going on," murmured Trixi.

"I bet it's something to do with that oyster," said Ellie angrily.

"I'll go down and investigate!" Jasmine announced. She ran to the nearest flume.

"Wait for me!" cried Ellie.

Summer took a deep breath. "And me!" She had to help find out what was going on!

Jasmine flung herself down the nearest slide. Ellie and Summer followed. They whizzed round the bends, faster and faster, and then with loud splashes they landed in the water. They only stayed underwater for a few seconds before they had to surface.

"Ouch!" squeaked
Summer,
holding her
hands to her
ears. "What
is that
horrible noise
in the water?"

"It's like
someone shrieking,"
Ellie said, shaking her head to try and get
rid of the sound.

"I think it was coming from Queen
Malice's oyster." Jasmine frowned. "I'm
going to check it out." She dived down
again and surfaced a few moments later.
Her eyes were bright with anger. "It *is* the
oyster. Queen Malice must have cast a
spell to make it scream like that."

Summer saw that the dolphins were all swimming in circles and bumping into each other. "Oh, no," she said in dismay. "The sound is messing with the dolphins' sonar. With such a loud, horrible noise, they can't use their clicks to work out where they're going."

"We've got to get out of the bay!" said Splash. With a flick of their tails, he and Bubbles set off. The other dolphins followed, overtaking the two babies with strong swishes of their powerful tails.

"Oh, no!" Ellie gasped. "All of the dolphins are swimming away!"

The Giant Oyster

"We have to do something or the Dolphin Dances will be ruined!" said Jasmine.

On board the ship, everyone had seen the dolphins leaving. Elves were shouting and they could hear King Merry calling, "Come back, dolphins! Please!"

"We have to find a way to make that oyster quiet," said Jasmine to Summer and Ellie. "Let's try swimming down and shutting its shell."

"Good idea," agreed Ellie. She looked at Summer. "You don't have to come, Summer."

"No, I will," said Summer bravely. "I'm going to help."

Together, the girls dived under the water and swam towards the giant oyster. The shrieking noise made their ears ring. They swam round behind it and put their hands on its shell.

"Push," mouthed Jasmine, a stream of bubbles shooting from her mouth.

Ellie pushed with all her might. On either side of her she could see her friends straining as they tried to force the oyster closed. But it was no use. The lid didn't budge one centimetre and Ellie was running out of air. Summer's face was pink as well, and her cheeks were bulging out.

Jasmine pointed up and Ellie nodded. Together, they kicked off from the sea floor and shot up to the surface. Ellie's heart was hammering against her chest by the time she broke the surface next to Jasmine and Summer. She trod water, panting heavily while she caught her breath.

"Can you fix it?" called King Merry from the deck. His eyes stared anxiously over his half-moon glasses.

"Well, we haven't managed to yet," Summer admitted. She racked her brains. How could they shut it?

"What do we know about oysters?" Jasmine asked.

"They make pearls..." Summer suggested.

"People eat them..." Jasmine offered.

"That's no good." Ellie shook her head. "Trixi, can you do anything?" she asked. "Is there a spell that can help?"

"I don't know," Trixi said. "I'll try." She flew down until she was hovering beside them and then twisted her ring round her finger. "All right, here goes!" She called out in a clear voice:

"Oyster, now you've done your bit,
Shut your shell, it's time to quit."

There was a loud pop followed by a bright flash of light.

Hopefully, the girls stuck their heads in the water then quickly pulled them out again.

"Sorry, Trixi, the noise is worse," said Ellie sadly.

Trixi's shoulders drooped. "I'm sorry too. My magic's just not strong enough to break one of Queen Malice's spells."

Jasmine rubbed the side of her head. Something was bugging her. The feeling had started when Summer had

remembered that oysters made pearls...
"I've got it!" she shrieked. She saw the
look of surprise on her friends' faces.
Taking a deep breath she continued in
a calmer voice. "Oysters make pearls,
right?"

Summer and Ellie nodded.

"It starts with a grain of sand," Jasmine
explained. "As soon as sand gets into the
oyster, it shuts its shell. The oyster stays
shut, and over time the sand turns into a
pearl."

"I get it!" Ellie's eyes widened. "We put
some sand into the oyster's shell to see if
that makes it close!"

"That's brilliant!" breathed Summer.

"Let's see if it works," said Jasmine.

"Wait," Trixi said as she tapped her ring
again. "Hold out your hands." There was

a burst of light, and silver sparkles rained down on the girls' outstretched hands. As the sparkles landed they turned into three sets of stripy earplugs.

"Thanks, Trixi," said Ellie as they took them and put them into their ears.

Jasmine pointed at the water and said something. Ellie couldn't hear much at all but she guessed it was Jasmine saying they should go. She nodded, her heart pounding. Were they going to be able to shut the oyster this time?

Oh, please, Ellie thought as she dived down into the sea. *Please let Jasmine's plan work!*

A Sandy Solution

The shrieking noise was terrible under
the sea, even with their earplugs in. The
oyster shell was wide open and the noise
blared out like a very loud, high-pitched
fire alarm.

Jasmine began digging her hands in the
sand on the seabed. Ellie and Summer
swam over to help her. The shrieking
grew even louder, making it hard to
concentrate, but Jasmine forced herself
to ignore it. When each of the girls had
a large fistful of sand they swam towards

the oyster. The closer they got the worse
the noise became. Gritting her teeth,
Jasmine swam on and emptied her sand
into the oyster shell. Nothing happened.
The oyster was still screeching as loud as
it could. Summer threw her sand in next.
Then Ellie. Jasmine's head began to hurt
and her lungs felt like they were being
squeezed. She wouldn't be able to stay
underwater much longer. They needed
to get some air. Maybe her plan had
failed…

But, just then, the two halves of the
oyster shell started to move. Jasmine felt
her heart leap. With an explosive crack
the oyster suddenly
snapped shut
and the horrible
screeching

stopped. The friends
shot upwards and
broke through the
surface of the sea.

Jasmine gulped
in huge mouthfuls
of the salty sea air.
"We did it!"

"Has the noise
stopped?" Summer pulled out her earplugs
and stuck her head under the water.
When she surfaced her face was lit with a
smile. "It has! It's lovely and quiet."

Ellie whooped. "The plan worked!"

The mermaids started to put their heads
under the water. "It really is quiet again!"
Marika gasped, surfacing, her rainbow
hair swirling around her. "Oh, thank you
so much, girls!"

"Hooray!" shouted King Merry, leaning over the railing of the ship and waving.

The elves on deck all cheered as the mermaids surrounded the girls, hugging them.

"The best thing is you haven't just stopped the noise," said Marika.
"You're making

something beautiful out of Queen Malice's horrid plan." Marika smiled. "In a hundred years' time, there'll be a wonderful pearl in the oyster. Once we've taken it out we can add more sand and the oyster will make another

pearl. There will be beautiful pearls forever."

"And best of all, the mermaids and dolphins will be able to stay here in Dolphin Bay," another young mermaid with pink and blue hair piped up.

The dolphins! Summer realised something. "Where are the dolphins? They haven't come back!"

King Merry lifted his golden telescope up to his eye. "They're far out at sea, still swimming away," he said in alarm. "They don't realise the noise has stopped."

"We've got to do something!" cried Trixi.

"All aboard!" cried King Merry. "It's time to set sail!"

Ellie, Summer and Jasmine scrambled up the ladder and onto the deck.

"I'll help steer, King Merry!" Trixi said hurriedly, winking at the girls. She tapped her pixie ring and the ship's wheel sparkled with magic. As the anchor was pulled up the ship began to sail across the bay. The girls felt the wind sweep through their hair as they headed after the dolphins.

"Watch out, watch out, we're coming through!" King Merry cried as the mermaids dived out of the way in a flurry of tail splashes. The ship surged forwards. Trixi flew ahead of the ship on her leaf as they chased after the dolphins. Bubbles and Splash were a little way behind the other dolphins, so the ship caught up with them first.

"Stop! Stop!" Trixi cried, swooping down in front of them.

The baby dolphins stopped in surprise.

"The noise has gone!" said Trixi. "All of the dolphins can come back. We must tell them."

Bubbles and Splash looked relieved. "Wait!" they cried to the other dolphins, but they just swam on.

"They probably can't hear us," said Summer. "My ears are still ringing from the noise."

"We've got to do something!" said Jasmine.

"Oh, dearie me." King Merry rubbed his nose anxiously. "I can't take the ship any closer. I might hurt the dolphins if I sail into their pod."

"If only the mermaids were with us they could swim after them," said Summer, looking back into the bay where the mermaids were waiting anxiously.

"The mermaids might not be here, but we are!" said Jasmine. "We can go after them!"

The three girls raced to the top of the tallest flume. One at a time they shot down it, keeping their elbows tucked in

to make them slide
faster until they
splashed into
the water.
Jasmine
swam ahead,
slicing
through the
waves in a
front crawl.
Ellie chased
after her and Summer

followed a short way behind. Suddenly,
Summer felt a dolphin swim up beside
her. It was Bubbles. She nudged Summer
with her nose and Summer realised
what she wanted her to do. She grabbed
hold of Bubbles' fin and the dolphin
started pulling her through the water!

At first they went slowly but then Bubbles started to speed up. Summer clung to her fin, the water spraying up around her. It felt like she was flying!

They raced past Jasmine and Ellie, who watched with open mouths. Summer grinned but didn't dare take a hand away to wave.

"Stop!" whistled Bubbles to her family and friends. "Please, stop!"

"Come back to Dolphin Bay!" called Summer.

Bubbles raced on and reached the other dolphins, who whistled in surprise when they saw Summer. As Bubbles swooshed to a stop, Summer let go. "It's all right — the noise has stopped," she told them breathlessly.

Ellie, Jasmine and Splash came racing up behind them.

"Summer's right. The bay's back to normal," said Ellie. The three girls began to swim amongst the frightened dolphins, stroking their hands along their smooth bodies to soothe them. One by one the dolphins started to listen.

"What's happened?" whistled the lead dolphin. "Has the noise really stopped?"

"Yes, we've shut the oyster," Jasmine

explained. "The sound has gone."

"Please come back to the bay with us," Ellie begged.

"Everyone wants to see you dance," said Summer.

The leader opened his mouth in a big dolphin grin. The other dolphins whistled and clicked in delight. "Then we'll come back!" said the leader. "Thank you so much for saving the bay!" Summer giggled as their smooth bodies flicked past her and dolphin after dolphin touched their snout to her nose, saying thank you in their own special way. She tried to copy their happy clicks and they grinned at her.

"We'll go back to the bay now," whistled the leader.

Arching their backs, the dolphins turned

and headed back
for the bay,
diving in and
out of the
water with sea
drops flying from
their skin like sparkling diamonds.

"Wheee!" whistled Bubbles and Splash
as they raced after them.

Ellie, Jasmine and Summer swam more
slowly back to the ship and climbed
aboard. Trixi magicked them some big
fluffy towels to wrap around themselves
and King Merry was so happy he did
a little jig on the deck. "You saved the
day, girls! You stopped the dolphins from
swimming away. Oh, thank you! Thank
you so much! Now the Dolphin Dances
can happen after all!"

Summer watched the dolphins swimming around the bay. She'd always wanted to swim with dolphins, but she'd never imagined being pulled through the water by one. It had been amazing! She remembered how all the dolphins had nudged and nuzzled her and the others and she glowed with happiness. She was never going to forget it.

"I wish you could stay here forever, but I'm afraid I think it's time for you to go home now," said Trixi.

Summer's face fell. "Oh." She'd really wanted to see the dolphins do their dances. Ellie and Jasmine looked just as disappointed.

"I wish we could stay longer," said Jasmine hopefully.

"Me too," said Summer. "I'd have loved

to see the dolphins dance."

King Merry clapped his hands together.
"Then so you shall! They're only going to
be practising today. Why don't you come
back tomorrow? You can see the Dolphin
Dances, and then we'll have a party to
celebrate."

"Oh, yes!" chorused the girls. "We'd love
to come back tomorrow."

They couldn't stop smiling as they said
their goodbyes.

"I can't wait for the morning,"
whispered Summer happily.

"I'll send you a message at eleven
o'clock." Trixi tapped her ring. "See you
tomorrow!" she called.

"Bye, Trixi! Bye, King Merry! Bye,
everyone," the girls called as they were
whisked away.

They landed softly on Sunny Sands Beach with the Magic Box between them. Their Secret Kingdom swimming costumes had changed back to their normal clothes, their tiaras had gone and their hair was dry.

"Wow!" said Ellie. "That was a great adventure."

"The best," agreed Summer, smoothing her hair.

"And we've still got another adventure to come," beamed Jasmine.

"Girls!" Mrs Macdonald's voice called faintly from the campsite. "Lunch time!"

Ellie wrapped the Magic Box carefully in Summer's towel and the three girls raced back.

"There you are," said Mrs Macdonald, putting a plate of sandwiches on a picnic

table already piled high with food. "I hope you're hungry."

"Starving," said Ellie, reaching for a sausage roll.

"Good," said Mrs Macdonald. "And after lunch we'll all go for a swim in the sea."

"This is my best holiday ever!" declared Ellie.

"Mine too," said Summer.

Jasmine sighed happily. "And it's only just begun!"

Book
Two

Contents

Sunny Sands Campsite

"Phew!" gasped Jasmine, throwing herself down. "The sun's really hot today."

"Lazy bones," said Ellie, shovelling warm sand over her legs. "You can't give up now. We've nearly finished."

Jasmine looked admiringly at the enormous sandcastle that they had been building. "It looks brilliant!"

"It does," agreed Summer, sitting
back on her heels and admiring their
handiwork. "It looks like King Merry's
palace!" The three of them grinned
at each other as they looked at the
sandcastle's turrets and spires.

"It's just like the real one." Ellie grinned.
"Only smaller."

"Girls! I've got some ice creams for
you!" Ellie's mum appeared through the
gap in the hedge that led to the campsite.
She was holding three cones of swirly ice
cream topped with strawberry sauce and
a flake.

"Yummy!" said Ellie as they ran over.

"Eat them quickly," Mrs Macdonald
said, handing them out. "They're already
beginning to melt."

"Thanks, Mum!" said Ellie.

"Can we eat them down by the sea, please?" asked Summer.

Mrs Macdonald nodded. "Of course you can."

Holding their cones, the girls wandered down to the sea. The cool water lapped over their ankles as they ate their ice creams.

"I can't wait to go back to the Secret Kingdom today and see the dolphins dance," sighed Summer.

"What time did Trixi say she'd send us a message?" asked Ellie, trying to lick a blob of ice cream off the tip of her nose.

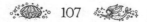

"Eleven o'clock," said Jasmine.

Ellie felt excitement bubble in her tummy. Visiting the Secret Kingdom while they were staying at the seaside was like having two holidays, not just one! "The Dolphin Dances sound amazing. I'm really looking forward to seeing them."

Summer smiled. "And I can't wait to see the baby dolphins again. Bubbles and Splash are so cute!"

"It's nearly eleven," said Jasmine, checking her watch. "Let's go back to the tent so we're ready."

The girls quickly finished their ice creams and washed their sticky fingers in the sea. Then they ran back to the tent, passing Ellie's mum and dad, who were busy playing beach cricket with Ellie's

little sister Molly and her friend, Caitlin.

Jasmine, Summer and Ellie hurried inside the tent and crowded into their small sleeping compartment.

"It's really warm in here," said Summer, fanning herself.

"We won't be in here for long," said Ellie, carefully lifting the Magic Box out of her sleeping bag. She ran her hand over the mirrored lid. Inside it were six magical gifts that had been given to the girls on some of their other adventures in the Secret Kingdom. As well as a magical map of the kingdom there was a dainty unicorn horn that let them talk to animals, a crystal that could change the weather, an hourglass that froze time, a special pearl that could turn them invisible and a little bag full of glitter dust

that could grant wishes.

"Look!" said Jasmine suddenly.

A bright light had started spilling from the sides of the box and shining words were forming in the lid.

Jasmine quickly read them out:

"Dear friends, please come,
now is your chance
To join us here, where dolphins dance."

"At least we know where we have to go this time," said Summer eagerly.

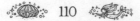

The three friends put their hands over the green gems decorating the lid of the box.

"Dolphin Bay!" they called out together.

There was a bright flash and a ball of golden light appeared and zoomed round the tent. It hovered over Ellie's green and purple sleeping bag before exploding into thousands of golden sparkles. When the sparkles cleared Trixi was there, hovering on her leaf. Today the little pixie was wearing a pink and yellow spotted swimsuit and a pair of sparkly pink sunglasses.

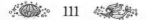

"Hello, girls!" Trixi said happily, zooming round and kissing each of them on the nose. "I'm so glad you got the message. Are you ready to go to the Secret Kingdom?"

"Yes, please," they chorused.

"Then what are we waiting for? Let's go!" Trixi tapped her ring and called out,

"Pixie magic, take us away
For fun and games in Dolphin Bay."

There was just time for Ellie, Jasmine and Summer to grab one another's hands as gold sparkles shot from Trixi's pixie ring and whisked them away. Ellie stared round dizzily as the magic set them down. This time they were standing inside an enormous stripy purple marquee that

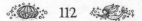

had been put up on a sandy beach. They
were wearing the same brightly coloured
swimming costumes as the day before,
as well as their tiaras. An enormous
chandelier hung from the pointed roof

and painted on the canvas ceiling
were pictures of dancing dolphins.
The tent poles were hung with shells and
strands of multicoloured seaweed and
there were several squishy chairs.

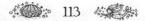

As the girls
looked around in
amazement, a
little snore came
from one of
the cosy sofas.
Jasmine peeked
round and saw the
kindly king snoozing on
it, his crown lopsided
on his curly white hair.

"King Merry!" cried Trixi. "We're here!"

The king gave a start and opened his
eyes. He beamed with delight when he
saw Jasmine, Ellie and Summer. "Well,
hello, girls!" he said, jumping up, his half-
moon spectacles slipping down his nose.
"Welcome back!"

"Thank you!" said Ellie.

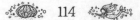

"We can't wait to see the Dolphin Dances," said Summer.

King Merry looked at his watch and jumped in surprise. "Goodness me, I must have dozed off. They should be starting any minute now," he told them. The girls stifled their giggles.

"Are you ready to go and watch?" the jolly king asked.

"Oh, yes!" they chorused.

"Then let's go!" King Merry declared.

The Dolphin Dances

"The best place to watch the Dolphin Dances is from a platform on the beach," King Merry explained as the girls and Trixi followed him out of the marquee. "This way!"

Outside they found the sun shining brightly. The crescent-shaped beach was packed with pixies, elves and brownies chattering excitedly as they waited for

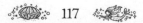

the dances to start. Music was playing,
and there were brightly coloured beach
towels laid out on the sand with parasols
beside them to keep off the sun's rays.
Everyone looked very happy. The bay
sparkled a beautiful turquoise colour
and in the distance the girls could see
the dolphins swimming about. King
Merry led the way up to a large wooden
platform, raised up above the beach to
give a view over the whole bay. On it,
there were four enormous cushions.

"Have a seat," said King Merry, settling
himself on the gold cushion in the middle.

"Can I have this one?" said Ellie,
carefully sitting on a squashy green
cushion with purple tassels.

"I like this one!" Summer said happily
as she climbed onto a red cushion

covered with pictures of unicorns.

"This is my favourite!" Jasmine sat down on a hot pink cushion covered with glittering multicoloured stars. "They're so comfy, aren't they?" she said.

Trixi gave a mischievous grin. "They're not just comfy. Up!"

The girls squealed and grabbed hold as their cushions suddenly floated up into the air. It was like being on a mini flying carpet!

"You can fly up or down to help you see the dance better," said Trixi. "If you say 'up' the cushions will go up and if you say 'down' they will come down. Easy!"

"Oh, Trixi!" beamed King Merry. "You are clever!"

It was great fun floating up and down on the cushions. The girls practised saying "up" and "down" while Trixi conjured up drinks for them all.

"Mmm, Starberry Crush! My favourite," said King Merry happily, smacking his lips.

The tall glasses were filled with a bright red punch and topped with pieces of star-shaped fruit, paper parasols and dolphin-shaped ice cubes.

Ellie took her drink and sipped it. "It's

delicious," she exclaimed. It tasted a bit like peach, passion fruit and strawberry all mixed together.

"Oh, look! There are Bubbles and Splash!" Summer nearly fell off her cushion in excitement as she pointed out to sea. The two baby dolphins were playing chase with three  other young dolphins, their smooth bodies shining as they leaped over the surface of the waves, turning and twisting.

"Bubbles! Splash!" Jasmine called.

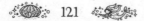

The dolphins heard her
voice and waved their
flippers excitedly.

"They've seen us!"
said Ellie. She broke
off as two brownies
suddenly played a fanfare
on golden trumpets. Out in the
bay the adult dolphins began to form a
large circle. The young dolphins swam off
to one side.

"The dances are starting!" said King
Merry in excitement.

Ellie put her empty glass down and
leaned forward to watch. "Will Bubbles
and Splash join in?"

"No, they're too little," Trixi explained.
"But they'll watch and try and copy.
That's how they learn the moves."

The adult dolphins formed a perfect circle then leaped out of the water, arching their bodies and dipping their heads in a low bow.

"Hurrah!" cheered the spectators on the beach. The girls joined in clapping and cheering at the tops of their voices. As the applause died away the dolphins began to dance. Slowly at first, they dived in and out of the sea, spinning around each other. The dolphins' moves got faster as they flipped, spun and arched their bodies in time with the music.

Trixi explained the stories as the dolphins danced. "This one is about a dolphin who escaped from five sharks and the next one is all about a mermaid and a dolphin who became best friends…"

"Ooh! Look at that!" gasped Summer as the dolphins leaped up and danced across the surface of the sea on their tails.

Then together they dived down creating a huge white wave that reared up in the shape of a frothy shark. The dolphins leaped away and the shark shape dissolved. Seconds later they surfaced again, their silver bodies skimming across the surface of the water, this time in two figures of eight.

"That's so clever!" said Jasmine. "See how they just miss each other when they cross over in the centre. We tried dancing a figure of eight in my ballet class once and it was a disaster. Everyone ended up crashing into each other!"

The girls clapped enthusiastically. Summer noticed Bubbles and Splash and the other young dolphins practising their dance moves away to the side.

"Look!" she said. "That's so sweet!"

The adult dolphins dived down again. Through the clear blue water the girls could see them weaving in and out between each other in a complicated move with lots of tail flicking. Then suddenly they swam up, breaking out of the sea to leap high into the air all together, twisting over in a huge flip as they did so.

"That's the triple tail flip," Trixi explained. "It's the hardest one to do, but the dolphins use it to jump really high."

The young dolphins copied, but Bubbles couldn't manage the flip and she landed with a huge splash in the water. She surfaced, shaking the water droplets from her head and grinning before leaping up and joining back in with her friends.

Summer sighed happily. It was so amazing seeing the dolphins dance. The adults were now leaping up, arranging their bodies to make another shape.

"Oh look, it's a mermaid!" Ellie squealed.

Summer started clapping with the others, but stopped as she noticed something – a familiar vessel approaching from the mouth of the bay. She leaned forward to get a better look and her insides turned to ice. "No!" she gasped.

Her frightened exclamation made Jasmine and Ellie swing round to look at her.

"What?" Jasmine asked.

"Look!" Summer said, pointing anxiously. "It's…it's…"

"Queen Malice!" Jasmine exclaimed.

Ellie gulped. "And she's heading this way!"

Dolphins
in Danger

"Queen Malice is coming!" exclaimed
Ellie as the chariot headed through the
sea towards the baby dolphins. Queen
Malice cracked a whip and the killer
whale swam even faster. As the girls
watched, four Storm Sprites dived from
the chariot into the sea, and a deep, dark
shadow spread out in the water, heading
straight towards the baby dolphins.

"Look at that shadow," Ellie said to the others. "What is it?"

"I don't know, but it can't be good if Queen Malice has anything to do with it," said Jasmine. She waved her arms. "Bubbles! Splash! Move away!" But the baby dolphins didn't hear – they were too busy concentrating on their dance moves. Bubbles turned half a somersault before belly-flopping into the sea. Splash gave a delighted clicking laugh, totally unaware of the danger they were in.

Suddenly the Storm Sprites popped up above the waves, each holding a corner of the shadow. "It's a net!" Summer gasped.

"The Storm Sprites are going to catch the babies in it!" cried Jasmine, noticing how the Storm Sprites' beady eyes were fixed on the five little dolphins.

"Swim away!" Ellie yelled to the baby dolphins, but they were too busy trying to dance to hear her.

As the girls, Trixi and King Merry watched in horror, the Storm Sprites flapped up out of the water and threw the net over the five baby dolphins.

The babies panicked and swam in frantic circles, thrashing their tails as they searched for a way out. Splash crashed against the net and got his fin stuck. He twisted and pulled.

"We've got to help them get free!" said Summer.

"Sister! Stop it!" shouted King Merry angrily.

Queen Malice cackled loudly, bringing her chariot to a stop just behind the net. "So, did you think you'd seen the last of me? Well, you were wrong!"

The Storm Sprites shrieked with laughter.

"These dolphins are coming with me!" said Queen Malice.

"You're not taking them anywhere. Let them go!" cried King Merry, his nose turning red with rage.

The adult dolphins realised what was happening and started swimming across the bay towards the babies as fast as they could, clicking and whistling in anger. But before they reached the young dolphins, Queen Malice pointed her staff

at them. The sea in front of the adult
dolphins churned as she shouted:

"Seaweed grow, strong and tall.
Build me an invincible wall."

There was a loud
thunderclap and
suddenly a thick
wall of green
seaweed
erupted out
of the seabed.
It grew
upwards and
outwards,
creaking and
groaning as it stretched across the bay in
a long thick line.

The baby dolphins were on one side of the wall with Queen Malice and her chariot and the adults were on the other, trapped between the beach and the seaweed. The adults swam at the wall, furiously butting it with their heads but they couldn't break through.

Queen Malice swung the chariot round, sending up a spray of water. "The baby dolphins are mine, all mine!"

She was so busy laughing with the
Storm Sprites that she didn't notice what
one of the dolphins was doing. He had
swum away from the wall and then
turned back towards it.

Summer caught sight of him and
shielded her eyes from the sun with her
hand. "What's that dolphin doing?"

They all watched as the dolphin swam
at full speed towards the wall. When he
was several tail lengths away from it he
leaped out of the sea. Sparkling droplets
of water fell from his silver body as he
rose in the air.

Jasmine gasped. "He's going to jump
the wall!"

Ellie screwed her hands into fists.
"Please do it," she whispered.

Summer's heart was in her mouth but

she couldn't tear her eyes away.

Just then, Queen Malice thumped her staff on the chariot floor.

There was a deafening crack and the sea swelled, rearing up in a towering wave of water as the wall of seaweed grew suddenly taller. The dolphin hit it with his snout and splashed back into the sea.

Summer gasped, but the dolphin surfaced a minute later looking shaken but okay.

The Storm Sprites whooped in delight, jumping up and down and flapping their wings. Queen Malice cackled.

"No one gets the better of me!" Her voice rang out across the sea. "My killer whale has served me well but he grows old. He's getting slow and unreliable. I need new fins to pull my chariot and these little dolphins look perfect. They shall live in the moat of Thunder Castle and pull my chariot wherever I wish to go. Soon they won't even remember their families in Dolphin Bay."

"You can't do that!" Summer shouted, not caring how scared she was of Queen Malice. "We won't let you take them."

"Summer's right!" yelled Jasmine. "You won't get away with this, Queen Malice."

An evil smile spread across the queen's face. "I think you'll find I will. Even you pesky do-gooders from the Other Realm won't stop me. Say goodbye to your baby dolphins!" Queen Malice raised her staff to the sky. "Storm Sprites, bring them to Thunder Castle!" There was a loud bang and she disappeared from the chariot in a spray of water.

Stop Those Sprites!

The Storm Sprites whooped. One of them sat at the front of the chariot and grabbed the queen's whip, while the others started attaching the corners of the net to the back of the chariot. The adult dolphins were still frantically swimming beside the seaweed wall, trying to get to the babies.

"They'll never break through," said
Ellie sadly.

King Merry noisily blew his nose on
a large spotted handkerchief. "Whatever
are we going to do?"

"There must be some way of stopping
the Storm Sprites taking the dolphins,"
said Jasmine.

"Maybe we could swim out to the net and free them?" said Ellie.

"But it would take too long," Jasmine pointed out. "The sprites will be gone before we reach them."

Out in the bay the baby dolphins' cries grew louder. The Storm Sprites had almost finished attaching the net to the chariot.

"Poor Bubbles and Splash," wept Trixi, whizzing round in a panic on her leaf.

"Oh, if only we had more time," said Summer desperately.

"That's it!" exclaimed Ellie suddenly. "Summer, you've just given me a brilliant idea! We can use the icy hourglass from the Magic Box. It'll freeze time and let us free the dolphins! We just need the Magic Box. Trixi, can you get it?"

"Of course!" Trixi tapped her ring and called out hopefully:

"Magic Box, please now appear. Icy hourglass, we need you here."

There was a bright flash and suddenly the beautiful box appeared on the platform in front of them. Its lid flew open showing the six objects inside, each nestling inside a separate compartment. "You did it, Trixi!" Jasmine said in delight. Ellie quickly lifted out the tiny pink hourglass encrusted with ice and filled with tiny snowballs. It had been given to the girls by the snow brownies after they had helped them on Magic Mountain. When it was turned over it would freeze time while the snow fell through it. Everyone would freeze while the snow ran from one side to the other – apart from the girls. It would only give them a few minutes to free the dolphins, but it might be enough.

"Brilliant!" said Jasmine. "Let's do it."

"Trixi, is there any way you could make our cushions fly across the sea to take us closer to the chariot?" Ellie asked.

Trixi nodded. "Easy!" She tapped her ring.

"Cushions fly across the bay
And stop the sprites from getting away!"

"Oh, well done Trixi!" cried the king as the cushions floated forwards. "Girls, get ready to go!"

The girls grabbed the sides of the cushions and held on tight.

"Then let's go!" said Summer.

"To the chariot!" cried Ellie. "Thanks, Trixi!"

The cushions gathered speed and started skimming over the surface of the waves towards the chariot. Jasmine held on tightly to the icy hourglass as the cushions soared up and over the huge, slimy seaweed wall. It would be awful if she dropped it! The Storm Sprites were busy climbing back onto the chariot, but as they flew nearer, one of them noticed the girls.

"Look!" he shrieked.

"Go away!" the other sprites howled as the girls skimmed towards them on the colourful cushions. "You can't stop us!"

"That's what you think," Jasmine muttered. "Ready?" she called to the others as the cushions reached the chariot and stopped, hovering above the water.

"Ready!" they gasped.

Jasmine lifted the icy hourglass and
tipped it upside down. As she did so, one
of the Storm Sprites opened his mouth
in rage and leaped towards her — but
it was too late. The icy hourglass had
frozen time and the sprite was stuck with
his mouth open and his wings stretched
out in midair. A second Storm Sprite was
frozen bent double as he stooped to pick
up the net. His nose was almost touching
his feet, and his bottom was stuck up in
the air. Jasmine couldn't help giggling.

"Well, they won't be causing any more trouble for now!" she said. Her voice echoed across the bay. The air was suddenly silent. It felt funny to look around and see everyone frozen still – the people watching on the beach, the baby dolphins in the net, the king and Trixi. Even the seagulls flying above the water had frozen in mid-flight.

"We've got to hurry," Summer called. "The poor babies!" She took a deep breath and slid into the water, her heart pounding.

"We don't have long before the spell wears off," said Ellie, following her.

"Wait for me," called Jasmine as she balanced the hourglass carefully on her cushion and dived after them. "We have to save the dolphins – and fast!"

∽A Daring Rescue∾

Jasmine, Summer and Ellie dived down underneath the chariot. The dolphins were all frozen, still bunched up at the back of the net, looking scared. The girls grabbed hold of the netting and their eyes met. They knew what they had to do.

Pull! Jasmine tried to say, a stream of bubbles leaving her mouth.

They all pulled together, struggling
to free the net from the chariot. At first
nothing happened, but then Jasmine felt it
start to shift.

She was running out of breath, but they
had to free the dolphins. They all heaved
again. The net didn't come free but it
started to rip. Jasmine's heart lifted, but
she couldn't stay underwater any longer.
She needed to breathe.

She shot upwards,
followed by the
others. They
gulped in huge
breaths. "The
net's tearing!" said
Jasmine excitedly. "If
we go down again and pull
really hard we might be able to make a

hole big enough for the dolphins to swim
through!"

Summer and Ellie nodded eagerly and
after taking in big breaths of air they all
dived down again. Taking hold of the net
beside the small hole, they pulled and
pulled…and the net ripped!

Soon the hole was big
enough for the baby
dolphins to swim
through. Ellie
gave the others
a thumbs up
and kicked her
feet to swim
up. They burst
through the surface
and grinned at each
other.

"We did it!" gasped Summer.

"And just in time.
The time spell's
wearing off,"
said Jasmine,
looking up at
the hourglass
on her cushion.
Only a few balls
of snow were left
and already the baby

dolphins and Storm Sprites were slowly
unfreezing.

The girls ducked down beneath the
water to watch as the dolphins unfroze.
The baby dolphins were starting to swim
round in the net, but they hadn't realised
there was a hole. They bumped into each
other, getting more and more panicked.

Jasmine stuck her head back out of the
water. "They can't find the way out!" she
said in dismay.

"Watch out!" yelled Ellie as the Storm
Sprite above Jasmine unfroze and
swooped towards her.
Jasmine dodged
to one side,
ducking
away
from his
outstretched
fingers. All
around them
were screeches and
shouts. The people on the beach were
yelling too, urging them on. The Storm
Sprites flapped over to the nearby wall,
ripping off great clumps of seaweed.

They started throwing it at the girls as they floated in the water. "Go away!" they shrieked. "We've got the dolphins! We're going back to Thunder Castle!"

The sprite who had leaped at Jasmine flew to the front of the chariot, grabbed the reins and cracked the whip. The killer whale started to move, dragging the chariot and the net behind it.

"No! We've got to show the dolphins how to get out!" gasped Summer. She dived down.

Ellie was about to follow her when Jasmine grabbed her arm. "The Storm Sprites don't know we've opened the net. We should distract them and give Summer a chance to help the dolphins get away." She and Ellie both ducked as more slimy seaweed came hurtling in their direction.

Ellie stuck her fingers in her ears, pulling a face at the Storm Sprites. "You missed!" she yelled.

Jasmine joined in, darting through the
water, taunting the Storm Sprites. "You'll
never hit me with that seaweed! You're as
slow as snails!" *Hurry up, Summer*, she
thought.

The sprites screeched furiously and
pulled more seaweed off the wall to hurl
at the girls.

Under the water, Summer was

frantically swimming
down to the
net. She
reached it
and pulled
open the
hole. To
her relief,
Bubbles and
Splash saw her.

Their eyes lit up and they stopped
swimming round in a panic. Summer
held the net so they could see the hole,
and with a flick of their tails the little
dolphins raced towards her, clicking and
calling to the other babies. One after
another, the five dolphins ducked out of
the hole as she held it open, her hands
gripping the net tightly as she tried to
make the hole as big as possible.

"Jasmine, look!" cried Ellie as Bubbles
popped to the surface.

"We're free!" Bubbles whistled in
delight.

"Quick, hide back under the water!"
gasped Jasmine. "Before the Storm Sprites
see you!"

Bubbles and the others dived away
with flicks of their tails.

"All right, all right we give up!" shouted Jasmine up to the sprites. "You win!"

"Yep, you can take the dolphins!" cried Ellie, swimming away from the chariot.

The Storm Sprites cackled in delight. "We win! You lose!"

"Silly slug-brained girls!" jeered one.

"You could never stop us!" shrieked another, his mean eyes gleaming. "You're too stupid!"

The one with the reins cracked the whip. "Let's get these dolphins back to Thunder Castle!"

The killer whale started to swim away. As the chariot dragged the empty net through the water the baby dolphins popped up around Jasmine and Ellie. "We're free!" cried Splash. "Oh, thank you!"

"Summer showed us the way out," said Bubbles as the other three dolphins frolicked around her in delight.

"Hang on." Jasmine felt like an ice cube had run down her spine. "Where is Summer?"

They looked round. There was no sign of her. They all dived under the water. She wasn't there.

Ellie swam to the surface and looked at the chariot. "Oh, no!" she gasped. "Jasmine, look!"

Just above the surface of the water they could see Summer's head and her blonde hair as she was dragged along behind the chariot. One of her hands was tangled in the net! "Help!" she cried, looking desperately over her shoulder. "Jasmine! Ellie! Help!"

Saving Summer

"Summer!" yelled Jasmine and Ellie, swimming after her as fast as they could. But it was no use. They would never be able to swim fast enough to catch the chariot.

"What are we going to do?" Jasmine cried.

"I know!" cried Bubbles. "Wait here!"

The girls turned and watched as Bubbles
and Splash streaked towards the wall,
aiming for the bit where the sprites had
been ripping seaweed away. It was much
lower than the rest of the wall.

Just before he reached it, Splash flung
himself out of the water in a flip. But
his jump wasn't high enough and he fell
back into the water.

"The wall's still too high," Ellie said
desperately.

Bubbles swam away from the wall.
With a gasp, Jasmine realised what she
was going to do. "She's going to try the
triple tail flip!" she told Ellie.

The girls held their breath as the brave
little dolphin swam up to the wall – and
leaped out of the water. They gasped as
Bubbles twirled in the air and flipped

right over the
wall!

"Hooray!
Well done,
Bubbles!"
Jasmine
and Ellie
cheered.
Seconds later,
Splash flipped
after her, and then both little dolphins
reappeared, jumping back over the wall.
But this time they were followed by one
of the adults, then another and another.
The air filled with angry clicks as one by
one the adults leaped over the wall and
surged through the sea, chasing after the
chariot and Summer.

"Hooray!" cried Ellie.

Suddenly the water by the girls parted and two dolphins popped up. Jasmine recognised them as Silver and Flash, two of the dolphins King Merry had introduced them to when they had first arrived at Dolphin Bay.

"Get onto our backs!" whistled Silver. "We'll catch the chariot and save Summer!"

Jasmine and Ellie grabbed the dolphins' fins and scrambled onto their backs. The dolphins were smooth and round and the girls had to hold tightly to their fins, their knees gripping the dolphins' sides.

Silver and Flash zoomed away through the water. Sparkling white foam sprayed up around them as they raced after the other dolphins and the chariot. Jasmine and Ellie clung on. If they hadn't been

so worried about Summer it would have
been great fun. The dolphins zipped
through the waves, getting closer to the
chariot with every second. The killer
whale was strong but the chariot was
heavy, and the dolphins were nearly
there…

"Faster!" shrieked the sprite who was driving the chariot.

"You're too late!" Summer managed to yell. "The net's empty! The baby dolphins have got away!"

"What?" the driver shrieked, pulling the reins hard. The killer whale screeched to a stop. The sprites stared at Summer in amazement. "What are you doing here?"

Before Summer could answer the adult dolphins raced up to the chariot, their usually friendly faces furious.

"So you thought you'd try and steal our babies did you, you horrible sprites?" whistled one.

"We'll see about that!" whistled another.

"Just wait till my teeth get hold of you!"

"Move it!" the sprites shrieked in fear.

Summer anxiously struggled to free her hand as the sprite holding the reins started to crack the whip, but the killer whale refused to move. As the dolphins raced closer, the cowardly sprites flew up into the air.

"Let's get out of here!" one yelled to the others as they raced away across the sky, their grey wings flapping.

"Summer!" Jasmine called as she reached the chariot on Silver's back.

"Are you okay?" Ellie asked as Flash swooshed to a graceful stop.

173

"Yes," Summer grinned. "But I'm very happy to see you. I thought I was going to Thunder Castle! I can't get my hand free."

Ellie slid into the water, carefully untangled her friend's hand and then gave her a big hug.

"I can't believe you rode dolphins!" gasped Summer.

Ellie patted Flash's smooth side. "Thank you so much for giving us a lift."

"Thank you for rescuing our babies," whistled Silver, nudging her big head affectionately against Jasmine.

"We'll make a new dance so that we'll never forget what you three girls have done," said Flash.

"Never," agreed Silver. "Your bravery will be part of dolphin history forever."

Jasmine, Summer and Ellie grinned.

"Bubbles and Splash helped too," said Ellie. "They were the ones who jumped over the wall and fetched you."

"We'll make sure everything is in the dance," promised Flash. "Now would you like a lift back?"

"Oh, yes please!" said Jasmine.

"Summer can ride on my back!" Another dolphin smiled at her. "My name's Kai."

"I'd love to have a ride," Summer said. "But first, can we do something about the poor killer whale?" She glanced

across at the miserable-looking creature.

"Let's free him," said Ellie.

She, Jasmine and Summer swam over to the chariot and started to undo the harness. He was huge but he stayed very still, his dark eyes blinking as he watched them unbuckle all the straps.

"There," Summer told him as they finally surfaced and patted his smooth black sides. "You're free. You'll never have to pull mean Queen Malice's chariot ever again!"

"Thank you," the whale said in a slow, deep voice. Then he blew out a grateful stream of bubbles and swam away, diving down into the deep with a flick of his tail. The chariot started to sink down into the sea. Queen Malice would never be able to use it again.

"Time to go back to the beach I think!" said Jasmine.

"And watch the rest of the Dolphin Dances," said Summer in delight.

Silver, Flash and Kai swam over and the girls climbed onto their smooth backs.

"Hold on tight!" Kai whistled to
Summer.

She clung onto his fin. The next second
they were off, racing through the waves.

The wind whipped Summer's hair back and the water droplets sprayed over her body and face but she didn't care. She was riding a dolphin!

The Grand Finale

As they swam into the bay Ellie realised there was still one problem. The huge slimy, seaweed wall stretched across the water, spoiling the beautiful bay. As the dolphins swam up to it Trixi appeared beside them, hovering on her leaf.

"Well done, girls!" She grinned happily.

"Trixi, is there anything we can do to get rid of the seaweed?" Jasmine called.

Trixi's face fell as she perched on top of the seaweed wall. "My magic's too weak to break it," she sighed.

Suddenly a fountain of water spurted up next to Summer. She looked over and saw the huge killer whale, his black eye staring up at her. "Maybe I can help," he said in his slow voice.

The water sploshed as he turned round, then smashed his huge tail against the wall. Trixi flew up into the air as the seaweed shook and crumbled.

"It's working!" Jasmine grinned. One by one the dolphins copied, bashing the seaweed with their tails. With every sweep of the killer whale's tail the wall got smaller and smaller, until it had broken down completely.

"The seaweed will feed the fish in the bay all summer long," Trixi grinned.

"Thank you!" the girls called to the killer whale. He waved his tail once more, then sank down into the deep water.

Clicking in joy, the dolphins started swimming in wide circles right around Dolphin Bay. Jasmine, Summer and Ellie laughed as their dolphins swam past the celebrations to drop them off at the beach.

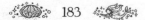

King Merry was standing by the
water's edge, looking very relieved. "Well
done, girls," he spluttered as the dolphins
reached the shallows and the girls
climbed off their backs. "I can't believe
you've saved the Secret Kingdom again."

"I don't know how we'd manage
without you," said Trixi, hovering beside
them on her leaf.

Two small grey shapes came racing

through the water. Bubbles and Splash burst out and flipped over in excitement before splashing down beside the three girls. "You did it!" whistled Splash. "You saved us and got rid of the sprites."

"We didn't do it on our own," said Summer, hugging Splash. "You both helped."

"You were brilliant," said Jasmine.

Bubbles and Splash looked delighted.

"Now we can watch the rest of the dances in peace, I hope!" said King Merry. He signalled to his trumpeters who called out a loud fanfare again. "Let's all get ready."

"First, Your Majesty, could we have a little bit of time to practice a new dance we would like to add on at the end?" said Silver.

"Of course!" said the king. "A new dance! How exciting! Take all the time you need."

The girls sat with King Merry and told him everything that had happened out in the sea.

"Dearie me," he said, shaking his head and making his glasses wobble. "Oh, my goodness. What will my sister think up next?"

At last the dolphins were ready. The adult dolphins formed a circle again. The babies swam in a group around the outside looking very excited. They kept whistling to each other and flicking their tails, completely recovered from their scary adventure.

There was another loud fanfare and the dances began again.

The adult dolphins twirled and spun in the water. They repeated the same dances as before.

Summer, Jasmine and Ellie clapped and cheered along with all the other spectators as the dolphins moved towards their grand finale.

"It's the new dance about the adventure today!" cried Trixi as some of the dolphins formed a long line across the bay. "They're pretending to be the seaweed wall."

While most of the adults stayed on one side of the wall, the babies raced to the other side and formed a tight group. "The babies are pretending to be in a net!" realised Ellie.

"And they're us!" said Jasmine in delight, pointing to three dolphins who were racing towards them.

The dance got faster and faster as Bubbles and Splash raced away and jumped over the backs of the dolphins who were acting the part of the wall. Everyone cheered. Bubbles and Splash led the adult dolphins back over the

wall. One by one they each flew over it, turning a flip or somersault.

The music built to a crescendo as all the dolphins leaped into the air, turning a perfect triple tail flip together. They ended the show by walking across the surface of the sea on their tails in a long line, and bowing low to King Merry and the girls.

"Bravo!" the king shouted, clapping so enthusiastically he almost fell off his cushion.

"Oh, that was brilliant," said Summer as the cheers finally faded and the dolphins dived deep into the sea to go and play.

"It was the best show ever," Ellie agreed.

Two little heads popped out of the water nearby. "Did you really enjoy it?" asked Bubbles.

"We loved it!" Jasmine said.

"Will you come back next year and see it again when we've added even more to it," said Splash.

"We'd love to – if we're invited," said Summer hopefully.

"Of course you will be," declared King Merry. "You are our very special friends. The kingdom will always welcome you." He sighed. "And we'll need you as well if my sister has her way. Something tells me she's going to be up to no good again very soon."

Jasmine smiled at him. "Any time you want us, just send us a message."

"We'll come straight away," said Ellie.

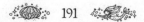

"We promise," agreed Summer.

"Thank you girls. I don't know what we'd do without you. Goodbye, until next time," said King Merry.

The girls held hands as Trixi tapped her ring. "Goodbye, King Merry! Goodbye, Trixi! Goodbye, Bubbles, Splash and everyone!" the girls cried as a glittering light surrounded them. "See you soon!"

The girls landed with a soft bump back on Ellie's green and purple sleeping bag.

For a moment they sat blinking at each other.

"Wasn't that amazing!" Jasmine breathed.

"Really exciting," said Ellie. "Two adventures in two days. Wow!"

"The dolphins were so gorgeous," said Summer, her eyes shining. "I'll never forget Bubbles and Splash."

"I don't think they'll ever forget us either," said Jasmine with a grin. "Not now they're going to do the 'Daring Dolphin Rescue' dance every year!"

"Girls!" Mrs Macdonald called from outside the tent.

"We're here, Mum!" shouted Ellie. "Just coming!"

They hid the Magic Box in Ellie's sleeping bag and left the tent. Mr and Mrs Macdonald were outside with Molly and Caitlin.

"There you are, girls," said Mrs Macdonald. "We've been talking and we've got a special treat planned for after lunch. How would you like to visit the local sea life sanctuary?"

"That would be great," said Jasmine.

"Yippee!" cried Molly and Caitlin jumping up and down.

"You'll even get to see some real, live dolphins there," said Mr Macdonald. "Won't that be exciting?"

Ellie, Summer and Jasmine exchanged grins. If only he knew!

"Oh, yes, Dad," Ellie said, winking at the others. "It really will!"

In the next Secret Kingdom adventure, Ellie, Summer and Jasmine visit

Wildflower Wood

Read on for a sneak peek...

An Amazing Adventure

"Look how long this is!" exclaimed Jasmine Smith. She held up the daisy chain she was making. "I'm going to turn it into a necklace for Summer. Butterflies will love her!"

"She'll like that!" Ellie Macdonald giggled as she flopped down on Jasmine's lawn. Their friend Summer Hammond loved all animals, and Ellie knew she'd be pleased to have butterflies fluttering all around her.

"Where is she anyway?" Jasmine asked. "She should have been here half an hour ago." She looked down her long, narrow garden, past the flowerbeds and the old apple tree to the back gate, but there was no sign of their friend. Laying the daisy chain carefully on the lawn, she sprinted down the garden, her long black hair streaming out behind her. "I'll see if she's coming," she called over her shoulder.

Ellie put her daisy chain beside Jasmine's and skipped after her. "I hope she gets here soon," she said, tucking a loose strand of curly red hair behind one ear.

Jasmine opened the gate, then jumped

back as Summer raced up on her bike, her blonde pigtails flying. "Sorry I'm late," she panted. "I was looking for my fairy tale book. I can't find it anywhere, and I'd promised my brother Finn I'd read him a story from it. He was really disappointed."

"Oh no!" said Ellie. "Can you remember where you had it last?"

Summer leaned her bike against the fence, then followed Ellie and Jasmine back up the garden. "I know I had it at the Summer Ball." She lowered her voice. "When we were…you-know-where."

The three friends exchanged excited glances, thinking about the amazing magical secret they all shared.

Jasmine gasped. "Did you leave it—"

"In the Secret Kingdom?" Ellie finished

for her in a whisper, not wanting to be overheard. They were the only people who knew about King Merry's magical world and the girls wanted to keep it that way. When the Secret Kingdom had been in trouble, King Merry's Magic Box had found the only three people who could help – Summer, Jasmine and Ellie. Now his pixie assistant, Trixi, sent them magical messages through the Magic Box whenever they were needed.

Just the mention of the Secret Kingdom sent a tingle down Summer's spine. It was a wonderful place full of elves, mermaids and other magical creatures.

"Remember the dream dragons?" Ellie said excitedly.

"And the bubblebees," added Summer. "They were so sweet!"

"I wish we could go back," Jasmine sighed. "We haven't been there for ages."

"I wonder how Trixi is," Ellie thought out loud.

"It would be great to hear from her," Jasmine agreed.

"But it's sort of a good thing that we haven't heard," Summer pointed out. "Trixi only sends us a message if Queen Malice is up to something. And as we haven't heard from her, that must mean everything's okay there."

Queen Malice, King Merry's sister, wanted to rule the kingdom, and she was always causing trouble. Once, she'd even tried to turn the kindly king into a stink toad, one of the nastiest, pongiest creatures in the whole kingdom! The girls had had to collect six rare ingredients from around the kingdom to make the counter-potion to turn him back to his normal jolly self.

"I know," said Jasmine, "but I wish we could go back. I miss Trixi and King Merry."

"Me too," said Ellie and Summer together.

"And I'd love to see the unicorns again." Summer sighed.

"I keep checking the Magic Box," Jasmine said. "But there haven't been any messages."

"I suppose we'll just have to be patient and wait until we hear from Trixi again," Ellie said. She picked up her daisy chain and rested it on her curly hair like a crown. "This will have to do until I can wear my real tiara again," she added, laughing.

"Can I have a look in your room, Jasmine, just in case I left my fairy tale book here?" Summer asked.

"Course you can," Jasmine said. "Do you need a hand?"

Summer giggled. Jasmine didn't have that many books – she preferred reading music magazines because she wanted to be a pop star when she grew up. "No, thanks. I think I can manage!" she teased.

"It's lucky it won't take you long to look," Jasmine said, grinning. "It's too sunny to be indoors today."

Summer ran inside and upstairs to Jasmine's bedroom. The Magic Box stood on Jasmine's bedside table next to a framed picture of a dancer that Ellie had painted for Jasmine's birthday. Summer peered into the mirror on the lid, hoping she'd see a message there, but all she saw was her own reflection.

Sighing, she quickly searched Jasmine's shelves, but her missing fairy tale book wasn't there.

As she turned towards the door, a flash of light caught her eye. Glancing round hurriedly, she saw that glittery light was pouring from the Magic Box's mirror. "A message!" she gasped. "At last!"

Read
Wildflower Wood
to find out what
happens next!

Secret Kingdom

Be in on the secret.
Collect them all!

Enchanted Palace — ROSIE BANKS

Unicorn Valley — ROSIE BANKS

Cloud Island — ROSIE BANKS

Mermaid Reef — ROSIE BANKS

Magic Mountain — ROSIE BANKS

Glitter Beach — ROSIE BANKS

Series 1

When Jasmine, Summer and Ellie discover
the magical land of the Secret Kingdom,
a whole world of adventure awaits!

Series 2

Wicked Queen Malice has cast a spell to
turn King Merry into a toad! Can the girls
find six magic ingredients to save him?

Look out for the next sparkling series!

Series 3

Queen Malice has released six fairytale baddies into the Secret Kingdom. It's up to the girls to find them – before it's too late!

Coming Soon!
August 2013

Competition time

WIN!

A year-long family pass to

Enjoy a whole year of adventure and fun with your family with this great prize!

All you have to do is tell us (in no more than 50 words) why you love Secret Kingdom adventures so much!

We will put all your entries into a draw and one lucky winner will win this amazing prize for their whole family!

Send your entry to Secret Kingdom Sea Life Competition, Orchard Books, 338 Euston Road, London, NW1 3BH
The prize draw will take place on 31st October 2013.
Competition open only to UK and Republic of Ireland residents.
No purchase necessary. For full terms and conditions please go to www.secretkingdombooks.com

Good luck!

Secret Kingdom

A magical world of friendship and fun!

Join best friends Ellie, Summer and Jasmine at

www.secretkingdombooks.com

and enjoy games, sneak peeks and lots more!

You'll find great activities, competitions, stories and games, plus a special newsletter for Secret Kingdom friends!